Judy Moody's Thrill-a-delic Hunt for BIGFOOT

WITH THANKS TO FIELD RESEARCHERS

Jamie Michalak and Kate Fletcher, *writers*

Mark Fearing, *illustrator*

Suzanne Tenner, *set photographer*

CANDLEWICK PRESS

WELCOME, BIGFOOT BELIEVER!

Since you are new to the world of Bigfoot, we'll start by learning all about Bigfoot and testing your knowledge. You can check your answers in the back of the book. Then we'll move on to tips and activities so you can work on your Bigfooting skills in the field. And finally — when you're ready — you'll learn how to go about tracking, finding, and catching the elusive beast yourself.

Let's get Bigfooting!

ACTIVITY: A HOAX?

Some people think Bigfoot does not exist—that he is simply a myth or, worse, a hoax. Match these animals, which were all also once thought to be made-up or extinct, with their description.

_____ 1. Saloa

_____ 2. Giant squid

_____ 3. Coelacanth

_____ 4. Komodo dragon

_____ 5. Platypus

_____ 6. Okapi

_____ 7. *Gigantopithecus*

Check It Out! If you're having trouble, or just want to see what those creatures look like, find pictures of them online or in an encyclopedia. Some are really strange-looking!

A. This large lizard wasn't discovered until 1956.

B. This fish was thought to be extinct for sixty million years—until one was caught in 1938.

C. Since being discovered in 1992, only twelve of these cow-like animals have been recorded alive!

D. This striped, giraffe-like creature wasn't found until 1900.

E. When this animal was discovered in 1799, scientists thought someone had glued the head of a duck to the skin of a mole.

F. Stories have been told of these large sea creatures since ancient times. Proof of them was finally found in 2006.

G. This was the largest ape that ever lived—ten feet tall and 1,200 pounds.

Activity: What Is Bigfoot? True or False

There are all sorts of theories about what Bigfoot could be. Read the list below and mark whether you think the statement is true (T) or false (F).

Some theories state that Bigfoot is:

A. __f__ an ancient giant ape

B. __f__ a cousin of the Loch Ness Monster

C. __f__ an alien

D. __+__ a large stuffed animal

E. ⌇⌇⌇ a Neanderthal

F. ⌇⌇⌇ a hoax

G. __+__ a very hairy person

H. __f__ a bloodthirsty monster

I. __+__ a bear

J. __+__ a person in a costume

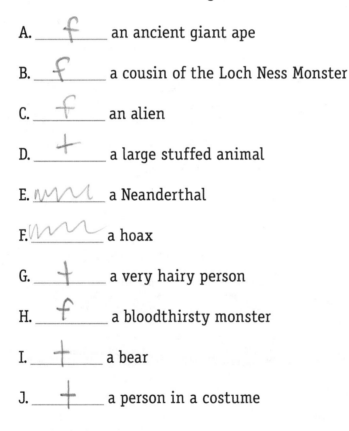

Do you agree with any of those theories? What do you think Bigfoot is?

ᴀᴄᴛɪᴠɪᴛʏ: Bɪɢꜰᴏᴏᴛ, Hᴇᴀᴅ ᴛᴏ Tᴏᴇ

To see how Bigfoot differs from a human, label each description with *BF* if it applies to Bigfoot or *H* for humans.

Head

_____ Has a sagittal crest, which is a Mohawk-like bump on the top of the head. No lips. Eyes are small, black, round, and set close together.

_____ No sagittal crest. Defined lips. Almond-shaped eyes with white scleras, colored irises, and small pupils.

Hair

_____ The body is covered in hair 1–4 inches long, especially thick on the shoulders and in long bangs over the forehead. Can be white, black, or brown, but most often a reddish color.

_____ Body often has short (1 inch or less), fine hair. The head is usually covered in longer, denser hair that ranges from pale yellow to black in color.

Skin

_____ The body is covered entirely with skin, which ranges in color from a pale peach to dark brown.

_____ Dark-colored skin is visible only on the face, hands, and feet.

Arms

_____ Long arms with large hairless hands and strong shoulders.

_____ Arms extend to mid-thigh with hairless hands and less prominent shoulders.

Stomach

_____ Often large and round.

_____ Ranges from large and/or round to flat with defined muscle.

Legs

_____ Range from strong to spindly with minimal to prominent hair.

_____ Strong and covered in long, dense hair.

Feet

_____ Average 11–22 inches long and up to 10 inches wide, with five toes.

_____ Average 8–12 inches long and 3–4 inches wide, with five toes.

ACTIVITY: BIGFOOT CHARACTERISTICS

Circle the words in the list that you think describe Bigfoot's personality. Then use a different color to circle the words that describe yourself.

Strong	Curious	Hairy
Bad-smelling	Ferocious	Athletic
Talkative	Gentle	Angry
Small	Weak	Shy
Silly	Smart	Good at hiding
Mean	Sensitive	Happy
Brave	Friendly	Silly

What characteristics do you and Bigfoot have in common?

8

ACTIVITY: BIGFOOT FAMILY LIFE

Read each statement about how Bigfoot families behave and mark whether you think it's true (T) or false (F).

A. _____ Bigfoot live in large groups of fifty or sixty, which are called Bigfeet.

B. _____ Bigfoot weigh between 80–100 pounds at birth.

C. _____ Young Bigfoot eat, sleep, poop, and cry.

D. _____ When a Bigfoot baby is born, the proud parents will invite guests over to visit.

E. _____ Bigfoot babies are able to walk within hours after being born.

F. _____ Young Bigfoot sometimes walk on all fours until they are six years old.

G. _____ Young Bigfoot like to climb, race, swim, play leap-frog, and uproot trees.

IN THE FIELD: BIGFOOT GAMES

Bigfoot of all ages like to play games to see who is the fastest or the strongest. Try some of these Bigfoot games with your friends or family. Whoever wins gets to be Bigfoot for the day!

Wrestling

Bigfoot, especially males, engage in full-contact wrestling. Set up an arm-wrestling tournament to see who has the most Bigfoot-like arm strength.

What you'll need:

> At least 2 competitors
> A table to arm wrestle on
> A judge (in case it's a close call!)

1. Divide into pairs. If there's an odd number, one person can be the judge and wrestle the winner next.

2. Both wrestlers should place their right elbows on the table and grip each other's hands.

3. When the judge says "GO," try to pin your opponent's hand to the table first while keeping your elbow on the table. Grunting, whooping, and other Bigfoot-like noises are encouraged.

4. Whoever gets his or her opponent's hand to touch the table first is the winner. If there are multiple wrestlers, the winners of each match then wrestle each other until there is only one winner left.

Winner: ﹏﹏﹏﹏﹏﹏﹏﹏﹏﹏﹏﹏﹏﹏﹏﹏﹏﹏﹏﹏﹏﹏

Jumping Rope

Bigfoot weave their own jump ropes from strings of bark or vines. You can use a ready-made jump rope, or make your own if you happen to have the proper materials handy.

What you'll need:

  1 jump rope (store-bought or homemade) per person
  1 or more opponents (optional)

For multiple people:

1. If you have more than one person, have everyone start jumping when you say "GO."

2. If you mess up or have to stop, you must sit down.

3. The last one jumping wins!

Winner: _____

For one person:

1. If you're competing against yourself, count how many jumps you can do before you have to start over.

2. Record the results below.

1st try: _____ 3rd try: _____

2nd try: _____ Best: _____

Tree Race

Bigfoot will race up to the tops of trees to see who is the fastest. You can race *to* a tree and back instead.

What you'll need:

Starting line
Tree (or other object to race to)
1 or more opponents or a stopwatch

For multiple people:

1. Pick a starting point and a tree to race to. You can make it as close or as far away as you like.

2. Line up along the start, then shout, "On your mark, get set, go!"

3. Run as fast as you can to the tree, touch it with one hand, and race back to the start.

Winner: ⁓⁓⁓

For one person:

1. If you're racing by yourself, use a stopwatch and see what your best time is.

2. Record the results below.

1st try: ⁓⁓⁓⁓⁓⁓⁓⁓⁓⁓⁓⁓⁓⁓⁓⁓⁓⁓⁓⁓⁓⁓⁓⁓⁓⁓⁓⁓⁓⁓⁓⁓⁓⁓⁓⁓⁓⁓⁓

2nd try: ⁓⁓⁓⁓⁓⁓⁓⁓⁓⁓⁓⁓⁓⁓⁓⁓⁓⁓⁓⁓⁓⁓⁓⁓⁓⁓⁓⁓⁓⁓⁓⁓⁓⁓⁓⁓⁓⁓

3rd try: ⁓⁓⁓⁓⁓⁓⁓⁓⁓⁓⁓⁓⁓⁓⁓⁓⁓⁓⁓⁓⁓⁓⁓⁓⁓⁓⁓⁓⁓⁓⁓⁓⁓⁓⁓⁓⁓⁓

Best: ⁓⁓

Ball Toss

Bigfoot love to throw rocks, but you can use water balloons (best in the summer), eggs, or even balls for this one.

What you'll need:

An even number of players

1 water balloon, egg, ball, or other object (not a rock!) for every pair

Measuring tape (optional)

1. Divide into teams of two.

2. Stand with your partner about 5 feet across from you so that there are two lines of participants.

3. On the count of three, toss the object to your partner.

4. If your partner drops it, your team is out. If he or she catches it, you both take a step backward.

5. Repeat steps 3 & 4 until only one team is left.

Winner: ⁓⁓⁓⁓⁓⁓⁓⁓⁓⁓⁓⁓⁓⁓⁓⁓⁓⁓⁓⁓⁓⁓⁓⁓⁓⁓⁓⁓⁓⁓⁓⁓

If there are only two of you, record how far apart you can get before you drop the object.

Best: ⁓⁓⁓⁓⁓⁓⁓⁓⁓⁓⁓⁓⁓⁓⁓⁓⁓⁓⁓⁓⁓⁓⁓⁓⁓⁓⁓⁓⁓⁓⁓⁓⁓⁓

ACTIVITY: BIGFOOT DIET

Bigfoot mostly eat plants, berries, and nuts. If food is scarce, they may eat fish and other creatures, but never humans. Fill in the food pyramid with the foods Bigfoot eat most at the bottom and those they eat least at the top.

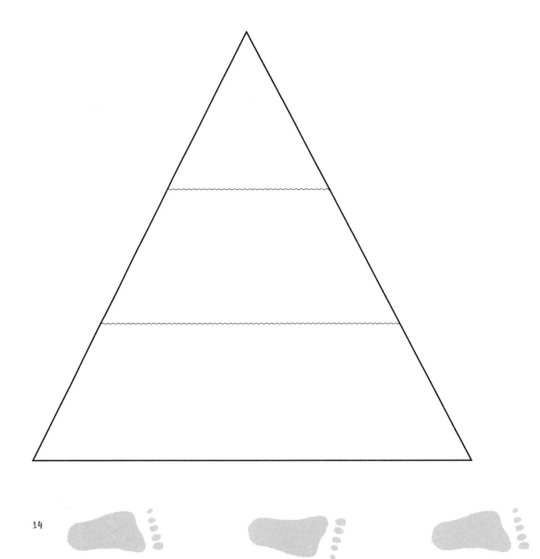

Now make your own food pyramid. Put what you eat most at the bottom and what you eat least at the top. Compare your diet to Bigfoot's. Do you like any of the same foods?

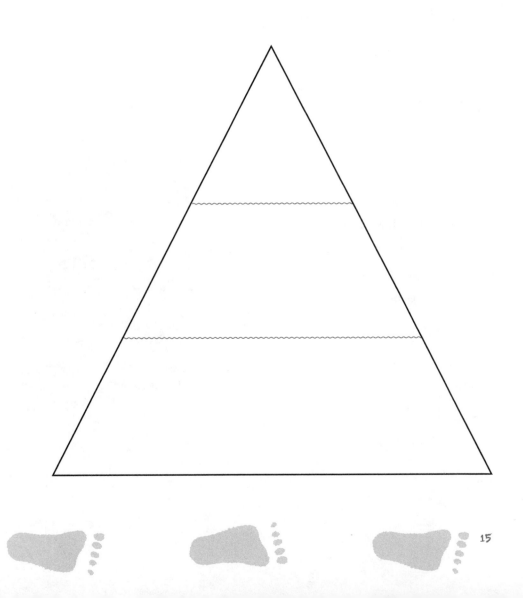

ACTIVITY: EAT LIKE BIGFOOT

This sandwich features Bigfoot's favorite food—peanut butter. Try it for yourself if you want to eat like Bigfoot, and be sure to make lots to use as bait when you build your traps (page 65).

Bigfoot Sandwich

What you'll need:

> 1 jar peanut butter
>
> 1 can tuna fish
>
> 2 slices of bread
>
> A handful of lettuce
>
> Some berries

1. Spread peanut butter on one slice of bread.

2. Spread tuna fish on the other slice of bread.

3. Add some lettuce to the top of the peanut butter.

4. Put both slices together to make a sandwich.

5. Eat with mouthfuls of berries for dessert.

Yum!

ACTIVITY: MAKE YOUR OWN BIGFOOT FOOD

Now you can make up your own Bigfoot-friendly recipe. List the ingredients and steps below, and be sure to make a few to test before you try it as Bigfoot bait!

What you'll need:

_____   _____

_____   _____

_____   _____

1. _____

2. _____

3. _____

4. _____

5. _____

6. _____

Taste-test results: _____

IN THE FIELD: HUNTING FOR FOOD

When other food is scarce, Bigfoot may go on the hunt to find prey. Rocks are their weapon of choice. They are also known to throw large rocks around just for fun.

Rock and Throw

Bigfoot can throw large boulders several hundred feet. See how far you can toss one!

Distance: Find a big area with lots of rocks. Mark off a line and stand behind it. Start by throwing small rocks and progress to larger ones. Measure the distance of your throws wih a tape measure. NOTE: *Make sure you've scanned the area for people or animals before you start throwing rocks.*

Accuracy: Pick a target (something stationary like a large rock or tree will work). Stand behind the line and aim for the target. How close can you come? Measure the distance between the target and your rock.

With a group: Get your friends or family and see who can come closest to a Bigfoot throw. Grunting or other Bigfoot noises (see page 52) may help to achieve maximum results.

Record the results:

Farthest: _____

Most Accurate: _____

Best Grunting: _____

target	rock size	distance	accuracy

Rock and Roll

When food is scarce, Bigfoot may hunt for insects or other small creatures underneath rocks. See what you can find by lifting up rocks of all sizes. Record your observations.

Location: ~~~~~~

Date and time: ~~~~~~

What did you find underneath the small rocks? ~~~~~~~~~~

~~~~~~

~~~~~~

~~~~~~

The larger rocks? ~~~~~~

~~~~~~

~~~~~~

~~~~~~

Do you think Bigfoot would eat anything you found? ~~~~

~~~~~~

~~~~~~

~~~~~~

Would you? ~~~~~~

~~~~~~

~~~~~~

~~~~~~

On the Hunt

Rarely, Bigfoot may simply catch prey and take it back to its nest, where it uses its foul stench to knock the creature unconscious. We don't recommend trying this. (Though, if you must, a stuffed animal can be substituted for prey.)

Activity: Bigfoot's Whereabouts

Bigfoot have been seen in all fifty United States and all Canadian provinces, but most Bigfoot live in the forests and mountains of the western United States and Canada. This area (which includes Washington, Oregon, and British Columbia in Canada) is called the Pacific Northwest. Find this area and color it in on the map.

However, Bigfoot have been spotted all over the country! Label or draw a line from these local names for Bigfoot to the appropriate area on the map.

○ Fouke Monster (Arkansas)

○ Lake Worth Monster (Texas)

○ Momo (Missouri)

○ Omah (Northern California)

○ Red-Haired Mountain Man (Eastern U.S.)

○ Sasquatch or Skookum (Canada)

○ Skunk Ape or Nape (Southern U.S.)

○ Swamp Goblin (Louisiana)

ᗗᑕTᏆᏉᏆTʏ: Bɪɢꜰᴏᴏᴛ Aᴄʀᴏss ᴛʜᴇ Wᴏʀʟᴅ

Bigfoot and Bigfoot-like creatures have been spotted all over the world for thousands of years. Match the name of the creature with the description.

_____ 1. Almas

_____ 2. Bigfoot

_____ 3. Mapinguary

_____ 4. Orang-Pendek

_____ 5. Yeti

_____ 6. Yowie

A. This apelike creature is found in the rain forests of Brazil and Bolivia. It has thick skin, a shrill scream, and a second mouth in the middle of its stomach. It feeds on cattle—and humans!

B. This creature walks with backward-pointing feet to confuse anything tracking it. It resembles a small human, thus its name means "little man." It is found in the jungles of Sumatra.

Check It Out! There's lots of information about Bigfoot and its kin out there (yeti footprints, scalps, and even an Alma's leg and skin). See what you can find online or in the library.

C. This white-haired creature ranges from 4 to 16 feet tall and is nocturnal and foul-smelling. It eats plants and animals and is found in the Himalayan mountains.

D. There is a larger (6–10 feet) and a smaller (4–5 feet) species of this creature. The smaller is not aggressive, but the larger is considered dangerous. Both are found in southeast Australia.

E. Its name means "wild man" in Mongolian and it most resembles a Neanderthal. These creatures are found in the mountains of Central Asia and often steal from mountain-dwelling people's homes.

F. Found across North America, especially in the Pacific Northwest, this creature stands between 7 and 12 feet tall, with a hairy coat and large feet. It is shy and non-violent.

Activity: Word Search

Bigfoot-like creatures can be found all over the world. Some of them and the countries they are from are listed below. Circle the names in the word search.

ALMAS (China and Russia)

BIGFOOT (United States)

FOUKE MONSTER (United States)

LAKE WORTH MONSTER (United States)

MAPINGUARY (Brazil)

MOMO (United States)

NAPE (United States)

OMAH (United States)

ORANG-PENDEK (Indonesia)

RED-HAIRED MOUNTAIN MAN (United States)

SASQUATCH (Canada and United States)

SKOOKUM (Canada and United States)

SKUNK APE (United States)

SWAMP GOBLIN (United States)

YETI (Himalayas)

YOWIE (Australia)

```
O N L M I P E P L E D C C E S X H B W F E Z N K O
E C B O V R F S T W B H W G T Q N F L F E O R R G
M V T I G R Y T E L J F I D S M I L J G E E G F P
D I D M P O O D I R P D G I P M G O V Q D I T L E
U X E L O U E R V S W N G H V S N Y P H H Q W L L
N R B Q A G L K E F M N B A F F V L A A A E V O V
Y Z T C L A G U C T F R X R R W D I M E E P R T Y
I X B D W H Z R E T S N O M H T R O W E K A L R H
S G B P K P Z Z Y S Y N M N K E D N E P G N A R O
H U I O R G R S O R K G O T D T S P D M S U B M J
B C E F H Q F I F E V O M M U B A D U W G I K V S
E M P O J Y Q N N P M W O J E S S L H N G I H P M
B S U S B S Y C T L Q U Q K N K Q X I F Y X K O N
S M F A C D S F L R N A V E U E U P O Q T Z B C F
K S W Z D P E W T T E S H N W M A O P Q L C A D P
W H U R R A J B A Q Y L K J K M T D F S E H P B L
V A A Y D Z V I A M Z A V Z E B C R Y C F S R T B
F Q U J F Z N W T C P N R C O V H X C W H R V V A
S C X H S M B M N E O G B H Y A S J B U E X V K V
Q S U B A G E T I F Y K O B M S H M I B O C P C F
C V Z N J P T E A T X W M B F P G O Q P L L U A M
R M B N E C A N X D H S M F L F Y A A O T O L I W
H Q V C M R D G G B K L U I Z I O Y K I D M I H G
R M W U I X X D I A E R Z N S B N Z L N A V P D H
F F A T U V P B Y J B O F S A B P B T S H C K X T
```

ACTIVITY: LOCAL BIGFOOT SIGHTINGS

To determine whether there might be Bigfoot in your area, find out if there have been any sightings nearby. Visit the library to search old copies of your local newspaper for articles. Ask a librarian to show you how.

Location: ～～～～～～～～～～～～～～～～～～～～～～～～～～～～～

Date and time: ～～～～～～～～～～～～～～～～～～～～～～～～～

Witnesses: ～～～～～～～～～～～～～～～～～～～～～～～～～～～～

～～～～～～～～～～～～～～～～～～～～～～～～～～～～～～～～～～～

Description of encounter: ～～～～～～～～～～～～～～～～～～～～

～～～～～～～～～～～～～～～～～～～～～～～～～～～～～～～～～～～

～～～～～～～～～～～～～～～～～～～～～～～～～～～～～～～～～～～

～～～～～～～～～～～～～～～～～～～～～～～～～～～～～～～～～～～

～～～～～～～～～～～～～～～～～～～～～～～～～～～～～～～～～～～

Check It Out! While you're in the library, read up on local Native American legends to see if any mention large humanlike creatures. You should also see if your library has books about Bigfoot. Check out the list on page 78 for suggestions.

ACTIVITY: INTERVIEW WITNESSES

Ask around to see if anyone has seen Bigfoot or knows of anyone who has. If you are able to interview the witness first-hand, you should!

Location: _____

Date and time: _____

Witnesses: _____

_____

Description of encounter: _____

_____

_____

_____

_____

_____

Check It Out! There are lots of Bigfoot sightings you can read about, including some by Norseman as early as AD 986 to one told to Teddy Roosevelt in 1893. Search the library or online to find out more.

ACTIVITY: MAKE YOUR OWN BIGFOOT DWELLING

Constructing different types of Bigfoot dwellings will help you to visualize what you will be looking for when you go out in the field, as well as offer you shelter when you are on a stakeout.

Create Your Own Tent Nest: Lay some leaves or branches on top of one another or weave them together to make a rough square. Prop this against a tree or bush. Line the ground with moss or grass to make it nice and cozy.

Create Your Own Tree Nest: Find a tree with strong-looking branches. Carefully climb up and perch yourself among the leaves and branches. Hold tight!

Create Your Own Den: In a cave or other dark place (a basement will do), gather leaves and sticks or blankets and pillows together to make a soft cushion.

Create Your Own Bigfoot Bed: Find a nice tree or bush, stomp around it to flatten the area down, and — presto! — you have a bed. You can also do this indoors with a comforter or blanket.

ACTIVITY: THINK LIKE BIGFOOT

Now it's time to start looking for Bigfoot! Remember that Bigfoot like woods and rocks, and need a water source. List some nearby places where you think Bigfoot might live and why:

ACTIVITY: FORM YOUR OWN BIGFOOT CLUB

Why not start your own Bigfoot club? Invite those you think have what it takes to be a Bigfooter, and don't be upset if they turn you down or even laugh at you. Keep trying, and you will find other Bigfoot friends out there!

List your members below:

Once you've gathered for the first time, decide how to organize and run your club. Have members vote on a president, vice president, etc., and discuss each person's duties within the club.

Name: ~~~~~~

Title: ~~~~~~

Duties: ~~~~~~

Name: ~~~~~~

Title: ~~~~~~

Duties: ~~~~~~

Name: ~~~~~~

Title: ~~~~~~

Duties: ~~~~~~

What is the goal of your club? Do you want to learn about Bigfoot, promote awareness, try to catch one, etc.?

Goal:

~~~~~~

~~~~~~

~~~~~~

~~~~~~

What is your club motto? (When in doubt, *In Bigfoot we trust* will always work.)

Motto:

~~~~~~

~~~~~~

~~~~~~

~~~~~~

Think about how often you'd like to meet and where. Set up a
schedule and location for future meetings.

date	time	location

It's important to take notes (called "minutes") at Bigfoot meetings to remember what was discussed. Have your club's note taker record the minutes below. (Copy these pages or make a club notebook if you need more room.)

Date:

Minutes:

Check It Out! The most famous Bigfoot organizations are The Bigfoot Field Researchers Association (BFRO) and the Bigfoot Society of America (BFS). Look at the BFRO online for sightings and other evidence. Read more about the BFS on page 72.

Date: ～～～～～～～～～～～～～～～～～～～～～～～～～～～～～～～

Minutes: ～～～～～～～～～～～～～～～～～～～～～～～～～～～～～

～～～～～～～～～～～～～～～～～～～～～～～～～～～～～～～～～～

～～～～～～～～～～～～～～～～～～～～～～～～～～～～～～～～～～

～～～～～～～～～～～～～～～～～～～～～～～～～～～～～～～～～～

～～～～～～～～～～～～～～～～～～～～～～～～～～～～～～～～～～

～～～～～～～～～～～～～～～～～～～～～～～～～～～～～～～～～～

～～～～～～～～～～～～～～～～～～～～～～～～～～～～～～～～～～

～～～～～～～～～～～～～～～～～～～～～～～～～～～～～～～～～～

IN THE FIELD: LOOKING FOR SIGNS OF BIGFOOT

Explore some of the areas you listed on page 33, keeping your eyes and ears open. NOTE: *Take a trusted grown-up with you or tell him or her where you are going first.*

Look for:

- Broken, snapped, or twisted tree limbs about eight feet up (which can only be made by a tall creature with enormous strength and a powerful grip.)

- Skittish animals (often observed when Bigfoot has been in the area.)

- Bigfoot nests, dens, or beds on the ground, in trees or caves

Be sure to note where and when you find any signs of Bigfoot and photograph them! (pages 58–59) ⁓⁓⁓⁓⁓⁓⁓⁓⁓⁓⁓⁓

⁓⁓⁓⁓⁓⁓⁓⁓⁓⁓⁓⁓⁓⁓⁓⁓⁓⁓⁓⁓⁓⁓⁓⁓⁓⁓⁓⁓⁓⁓

⁓⁓⁓⁓⁓⁓⁓⁓⁓⁓⁓⁓⁓⁓⁓⁓⁓⁓⁓⁓⁓⁓⁓⁓⁓⁓⁓⁓⁓⁓

⁓⁓⁓⁓⁓⁓⁓⁓⁓⁓⁓⁓⁓⁓⁓⁓⁓⁓⁓⁓⁓⁓⁓⁓⁓⁓⁓⁓⁓⁓

⁓⁓⁓⁓⁓⁓⁓⁓⁓⁓⁓⁓⁓⁓⁓⁓⁓⁓⁓⁓⁓⁓⁓⁓⁓⁓⁓⁓⁓⁓

IN THE FIELD: GATHERING EVIDENCE

As a Bigfooter, it's incredibly important to gather evidence to prove Bigfoot's existence. So always keep an eye out and be sure to record and report your findings!

Hair

Look in tree branches, bushes, and on the ground for tufts of hair that could belong to Bigfoot.

What did you find? _____

_____

Where? _____

When? _____

What makes you think it could be Bigfoot hair? _____

_____

_____

_____

_____

Compare it to other hair samples—your own, your pets', whatever you can find! Use a magnifying glass if you have one. Tape your hair sample onto the page below.

Similarities: _____

_____

_____

_____

Differences: _____

_____

_____

Hair sample:

Scat

You will know Bigfoot scat (poop) by its size — typically two to three feet long(!). Still, be sure to examine it carefully in order to ensure that it truly is Bigfoot's.

What you'll need:

Gloves
Tongs (or other poop-picking tool)
Several sealable plastic bags
A permanent marker
A small cooler
Nose plugs (optional)

1. In a Bigfoot-friendly area look on the ground around bushes or trees for scat.

2. Once you've found some, pull on your gloves, grab your tongs, and get that scat! NOTE: *Always wear latex gloves and use tongs (or a spoon, spatula, etc.) to pick up your sample. Use a nose plug if necessary.*

3. Place each scat sample in a separate plastic bag.

4. Label each with the date and location, as well as a letter (Specimen A, B, C, etc.).

5. Place the baggies in a cooler that you've clearly labeled "SCAT."

6. You can store your clearly labeled baggies in the freezer when you get home.

7. Study your specimens and record your findings.

NOTE: *It is not easy to find Bigfoot scat! So don't get disheartened if you can't find any right away, and don't give up! Bigfoot scat is an incredibly important piece of evidence, so follow your nose and keep searching!*

Specimen A

Location found: ~~~~~~

Date and time of finding: ~~~~~~~~~~~~~~~~~~~~~~~~~~~~~~~~~~

Length and width: ~~~~~~

Is there one dropping, or are there multiple ones? ~~~~~~~~~

~~~~~~

How old do you think the droppings are? (NOTE: *The softer the scat, the fresher it is—a clue for telling if the animal is close!*) ~~~~~~

~~~~~~

Describe the color and consistency, which are results of the animal's diet. Can you identify any hair or undigested food particles? ~~~~~~

~~~~~~

~~~~~~

Do you think this scat could be Bigfoot's? Why or why not?

~~~~~~

~~~~~~

~~~~~~

~~~~~~

Specimen B

Location found: ~~~~~~

Date and time of finding: ~~~~~~~~~~~~~~~~~~~~~~~~~~~~~~~~~~~

Length and width: ~~~~~~

Is there one dropping, or are there multiple ones? ~~~~~~~~~~

~~~~~~

How old do you think the droppings are? ~~~~~~~~~~~~~~~~~~~~~

~~~~~~

Describe the color and consistency. Can you identify any hair or undigested food particles? ∿∿∿∿∿∿∿∿∿∿

∿∿

∿∿

Do you think this scat could be Bigfoot's? Why or why not?

∿∿

∿∿

∿∿

IN THE FIELD: TRACKING BIGFOOT

The most common evidence of Bigfoot are their footprints. Look for prints near wet areas, where they will be most visible. Fill out this questionnaire to help you determine if it is a Bigfoot print.

Where and when did you find the footprint? _____

_____

How long is it? _____
(Bigfoot feet are 11–22 inches long.)

How wide is it? _____
(Bigfoot feet can be up to 10 inches wide.)

How many toes are there? _____
(Bigfoot feet usually have five toes)

Is the inside toe much larger than the others? _____
(Bigfoot have a large big toe.)

Is there a foot arch? _____
(Bigfoot have flat feet, so no arch.)

How deep is the print? _____
(Bigfoot prints should be about 3½ inches deep.)

Is there a mound of dirt mid-footprint? _____
(A Bigfoot foot creates a push of the forefoot just before it leaves
the ground, leaving a mound of dirt behind it.)

If you see more than one footprint, how much space is in
between them? _____
(Bigfoot steps should be at least 6 feet apart, tightly aligned in
single file.)

If you suspect the print is not from Bigfoot, examine human
and other prints to see if you can identify it.

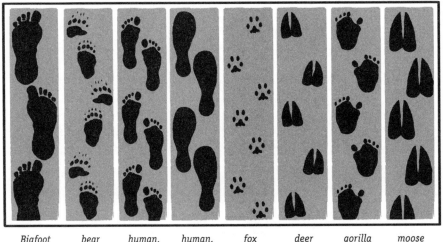

| Bigfoot | bear | human, barefoot | human, wearing clown shoes | fox | deer | gorilla | moose |

Activity: Cast Your Bigfoot Print

If you have determined that you have found a real Bigfoot print, be sure to document it properly with a plaster cast and lots of photographs!

What you'll need:
Plaster of Paris (the quick-drying kind)
Water in a portable container
Large bowl and spoon for mixing
Small shovel or trowel

1. Once you've found a footprint, carefully clear off leaves or other debris so you'll be sure to get a clean cast.

2. Mix the plaster of Paris and water in the bowl as directed on the packaging. Make sure to stir the lumps out completely. (NOTE: *When you're done, clean the bowl and spoon before the plaster hardens!*)

3. Pour the plaster of Paris into the track so that the print is totally filled and the plaster is at least one inch thick above it.

4. Either leave the plaster there to dry overnight or let it set for at least 45 minutes, then dig it up with the shovel or trowel — cast, dirt, and all — and take it home to dry completely overnight.

5. Once the cast has completely cured, carefully clean any dirt away from it and admire your Bigfoot footprint.

Be sure to share your discovery!

IN THE FIELD: BIGFOOT NOISES

Use your tape recorder to capture possible Bigfoot sounds, and then compare them to other animal and Bigfoot recordings.

Recording #1:

When did you hear the noise? ⁓⁓⁓⁓⁓⁓⁓⁓⁓⁓⁓⁓⁓⁓

Where? ⁓⁓⁓⁓⁓⁓⁓⁓⁓⁓⁓⁓⁓⁓⁓⁓⁓⁓⁓⁓

What did it sound like and how long did it go on? ⁓⁓⁓⁓

⁓⁓⁓⁓⁓⁓⁓⁓⁓⁓⁓⁓⁓⁓⁓⁓⁓⁓⁓⁓⁓⁓⁓⁓⁓⁓⁓⁓⁓⁓⁓⁓

⁓⁓⁓⁓⁓⁓⁓⁓⁓⁓⁓⁓⁓⁓⁓⁓⁓⁓⁓⁓⁓⁓⁓⁓⁓⁓⁓⁓⁓⁓⁓⁓

Do you think it's a Bigfoot noise? Why or why not? ⁓⁓⁓

⁓⁓⁓⁓⁓⁓⁓⁓⁓⁓⁓⁓⁓⁓⁓⁓⁓⁓⁓⁓⁓⁓⁓⁓⁓⁓⁓⁓⁓⁓⁓⁓

⁓⁓⁓⁓⁓⁓⁓⁓⁓⁓⁓⁓⁓⁓⁓⁓⁓⁓⁓⁓⁓⁓⁓⁓⁓⁓⁓⁓⁓⁓⁓⁓

⁓⁓⁓⁓⁓⁓⁓⁓⁓⁓⁓⁓⁓⁓⁓⁓⁓⁓⁓⁓⁓⁓⁓⁓⁓⁓⁓⁓⁓⁓⁓⁓

⁓⁓⁓⁓⁓⁓⁓⁓⁓⁓⁓⁓⁓⁓⁓⁓⁓⁓⁓⁓⁓⁓⁓⁓⁓⁓⁓⁓⁓⁓⁓⁓

Recording #2:

When did you hear the noise? _____

Where? _____

What did it sound like and how long did it go on? _____

_____

_____

Do you think it's a Bigfoot noise? Why or why not? _____

_____

_____

_____

Check It Out! Researchers have recorded all kinds of Bigfoot noises: grunts, howls, roars, whooping, and haunting cries. Familiarize yourself with these noises — as well as those of coyotes, wolves, bears, birds, and other animals in your area — before you head into the field. This will help you distinguish Bigfoot's call.

IN THE FIELD: CALLING BIGFOOT

You should learn what Bigfoot's noises mean and practice and perfect them. They are difficult to master, and you don't want to mess them up—the wrong call could spell disaster!

Call:	Meaning:
Whooooo Woo-OOP, woo-OOP, woo-OOP	This common call signifies that food is nearby.
Whistle	A six-second whistle means, "Do you want to play?"
Belch	Loud belching vocalizations let other Bigfoot know where they are located.
Aye-yi-YI!	A piercing, high-pitched, bloodcurdling shriek is a call of distress.
Coo, coo	Bigfoot's mating call.

IN THE FIELD: BIGFOOT SIGN LANGUAGE

Bigfoot also communicate using Bigfoot Sign Language. Practice and learn these key phrases so you can communicate with a Bigfoot once you've caught him or her.

I am your friend.

a disgusting smell or human

I will not eat/hurt you.

car

Run for your life!
or
GUINEA PIG!

Yes

Don't come any closer.

I am thirsty.

No

I am hungry.

When you have captured your Bigfoot or are communicating with one in the wild, try making up your own signs. Describe them below, what they mean, and Bigfoot's reaction:

Your sign	Meaning	Bigfoot reaction

Also be sure to record all of Bigfoot's signs, even if you don't understand them. They will be useful for later study and should be shared with the Bigfoot community.

Bigfoot's sign	What do you think it means?

ᴀᴄᴛɪᴠɪᴛʏ: Pʜᴏᴛᴏs ᴏꜰ Bɪɢꜰᴏᴏᴛ

Match the famous Bigfoot photo with its description.

_____ 1. *Mount Rainier Bigfoot, 1995:* This photo was taken by a forest patrol officer near Mount Rainier in Washington state. The officer was looking for bear poachers when he heard splashing sounds nearby. He peeked over a ledge and saw Bigfoot!

_____ 2. *Skunk Ape, 2000:* This was taken in the Florida Everglades, where Bigfoot is known as the skunk ape due to its powerful stench. The woman who took this photograph claimed the creature entered her yard at night to take apples from a basket on her porch.

_____ 3. *Jacobs's creature, 2007:* This picture was taken in the forests of Pennsylvania by Rick Jacobs, who was trying to photograph deer at night. Some people claim this is a sickly bear, but Bigfooters believe it shows a juvenile Bigfoot.

A.

© 2007 R. Jacobs

BUSHNELL   09/16/2007 20:32:05

B.

C.

57

IN THE FIELD: PHOTOGRAPHING BIGFOOT

While looking for evidence, you can also practice your photography skills. Be sure to take your camera with you at all times, as you never know when you might spot Bigfoot!

What you'll need:

A camera (either digital or film is fine)
Memory card or film

1. Head to the Bigfoot-friendly areas identified earlier and/or where you've found any evidence of Bigfoot.

2. While keeping an eye—and ear—out for evidence and noises, find some trees, rocks, etc., to photograph.

3. Play around with the different settings on your camera and see what the results are.

4. Once you've mastered photographing still objects, see if you can photograph a human or animal in low light.

5. Record the best settings for clear photos in different types of light:

If you happen to see Bigfoot, take as many photos as you can immediately! Don't wait for it to get closer — it probably won't, and you'll have missed your shot. Be sure to record where photographs were taken and when, and report your findings.

Time: _____

Location: _____

Description of encounter: _____

_____

(Paste photograph here)

ACTIVITY: VIDEOING BIGFOOT

Most digital cameras have a video feature, so get familiar with yours. Keep the camera as still as you can, zoom in close for details, and pull back to get motion shots.

Video #1:

    Time: _____

    Location: _____

    Description of encounter: _____

_____

_____

Video #2:

    Time: _____

    Location: _____

    Description of encounter: _____

_____

_____

Video #3:

Time: ︴︴︴︴︴︴︴︴︴︴︴︴︴︴︴︴︴︴

Location: ︴︴︴︴︴︴︴︴︴︴︴︴︴︴︴︴

Description of encounter: ︴︴︴︴︴︴︴︴

︴︴︴︴︴︴︴︴︴︴︴︴︴︴︴︴︴︴︴︴︴︴

︴︴︴︴︴︴︴︴︴︴︴︴︴︴︴︴︴︴︴︴︴︴

Check It Out! Watch the Patterson-Gimlin footage (taken in 1967 in Bluff Creek, California), as it is by far the most famous Bigfoot video and has never been disproved!

ACTIVITY: MAKE A BERRY-BUSH DISGUISE

When you're in the field tracking Bigfoot, you need to make sure you won't be detected. Wear camouflage or make your own disguise.

What you'll need:

> Glue
> Leaves
> Twigs
> Berries (any kind will do)
> Old hooded sweatshirt (large)
> Old baseball cap

1. Glue leaves onto the sweatshirt and cap.

2. Glue twigs onto the sweatshirt and cap.

3. Glue berries onto the sweatshirt and cap.

4. Let the glue dry completely before wearing into the field.

NOTE: *When on a stake-out, do not use or bring deodorant, breath mints, etc. Bigfoot have a keen sense of smell, and these types of smells will alert them to your presence and cause them to avoid the area.*

IN THE FIELD: PACKING FOR A STAKEOUT

It's important to be prepared before you head out on a stakeout. Use this list as a guide, but think about other things you might need as well. Be sure to double-check your bag before you head out!

What you'll need:

- ○ Tent
- ○ Sleeping bag
- ○ Binoculars
- ○ Nose clip (Bigfoot's smell has caused some to pass out.)
- ○ Video camera
- ○ Camera
- ○ Tape recorder
- ○ Supplies for building a trap (see page 65)
- ○ Supplies for gathering scat (see page 43)
- ○ This book
- ○ Equipment for making casts of footprints (see page 49)
- ○ Flashlight
- ○ Berry-Bush Disguise (see page 62) and/or camouflage gear
- ○ Meals, eating utensils, a thermos, and lots of hot chocolate

Other:

~~~~~~~~~~~~~~~~~~~~~~~~~   ~~~~~~~~~~~~~~~~~~~~~~~~~

~~~~~~~~~~~~~~~~~~~~~~~~~   ~~~~~~~~~~~~~~~~~~~~~~~~~

~~~~~~~~~~~~~~~~~~~~~~~~~   ~~~~~~~~~~~~~~~~~~~~~~~~~

IN THE FIELD: STAKEOUT!

Aim to go on your stakeout during peak season (June–July), though Bigfoot do sometimes come down from the mountains during winter as well. NOTE: *Avoid hunting seasons.* Write down the plan (goal, number of days, etc.) for your stakeout.

Date: _____

Location: _____

Plan: _____

_____

_____

_____

_____

NOTE: *Never track Bigfoot in remote areas alone. That's what your Bigfoot club is for! (see page 34) So be sure to bring along a fellow Bigfooter and let an adult know where you are going.*

IN THE FIELD: BUILDING TRAPS

Build your trap during the day, while Bigfoot are asleep, and then go on stakeout at night, when Bigfoot are out looking for food.

Try the trap described below or create your own on the next page:

The Peanut-Butter Trap

This simple trap is good for beginners. When Bigfoot grabs one of the peanut-butter jars, the attached net will fall and trap him.

What you'll need:

30 jars of peanut butter
30 pieces of string (3 feet each)
Net or hammock
Berry-bush disguise (see page 62)

1. Hang a large net from the branches of a tree. Make sure the netting is hidden among the leaves.

2. Tie the peanut-butter jars to the netting. They should dangle low enough for Bigfoot to see and reach.

3. Put on your camouflage or disguise, hide, and wait.

Check It Out! The world's only permanent Bigfoot trap is in the Siskiyou National Forest in Oregon. It hasn't caught a Bigfoot yet — that we know of, at least!

ACTIVITY: DESIGN YOUR OWN TRAP

Try designing your own Bigfoot trap. Describe it below and write down what materials you need and instructions for building it. Be sure to write down how you will release Bigfoot on page 71!

Description: ~~~~~~

~~~~~~

What you'll need:

~~~~~~~~~~~~~~~~~~~~~~~~~~~~~~~~~~   ~~~~~~~~~~~~~~~~~~~~~~~~~~~~~~~~~~

~~~~~~~~~~~~~~~~~~~~~~~~~~~~~~~~~~   ~~~~~~~~~~~~~~~~~~~~~~~~~~~~~~~~~~

~~~~~~~~~~~~~~~~~~~~~~~~~~~~~~~~~~   ~~~~~~~~~~~~~~~~~~~~~~~~~~~~~~~~~~

1. ~~~~~~

2. ~~~~~~

3. ~~~~~~

4. ~~~~~~

5. ~~~~~~

6. ~~~~~~

IN THE FIELD: On a Stakeout

Once your trap is built and you have disguised and hidden yourself, it's time to watch and wait. Here are a couple of activities to fill the hours. Bigfoot-related reading (see page 78) is also recommended.

Your Biography

This is a good time for you to work on a short biography. If and when you do catch Bigfoot, you will become famous very quickly, so you'll want to have a bio ready. Use the biography of famous Bigfooter Morgan Jackson as a guide:

 **Morgan Jackson, PhD (1991–)** is a self-taught Bigfoot researcher who has followed the creature across North America and had more than fifty Bigfoot encounters. His contributions to the field include the groundbreaking discovery of Bigfoot Sign Language.

Sudoku

You can also pass the time playing sudoku. The goal of sudoku is to make sure every line (both vertical and horizontal) and every 3 x 3 grid contains each number from 1 to 9.

	8	3	1		5	6	4	
7								5
5		1	2		8	3		7
2								3
	3	6	8		7	5	2	
8								1
3		2	4		9	1		8
6								4
1	4	7	3		2	9	5	

IN THE FIELD: CAUGHT!

When you succeed in capturing Bigfoot, reassure him with sign language (see page 53) and soothing noises (see page 52). Record everything—how you caught him, what he looks like, sounds like, smells like, as well as all of your communication. Be sure to video as much as possible!

☞IN THE FIELD: GATHERING PROOF

It's likely Bigfoot will grow weary of communicating after what will seem like a short period of time. This is the time to go about collecting evidence.

Follow the checklist below:

○ Take photos from all angles of Bigfoot at rest, communicating, eating, etc.

○ Take video of Bigfoot communicating and in motion.

○ Make casts of any footprints around the trap.

○ Collect any hair or scat in the area.

○ Record everything! No detail is too small for a Bigfooter!

IN THE FIELD: Release and Good-Bye

Now it's time to let your Bigfoot go. Take a deep breath, sign good-bye, and proceed to release him from the trap. How you release him will depend on what type of trap you've built.

Peanut-Butter Trap
Untie several jars of peanut butter from the net and roll them over to Bigfoot. While he's distracted, pull the net off and throw more jars as far away as you can to lead him away from you.

Your Own Trap

⬛ IN THE FIELD: TIME TO GO

But be sure to follow the proper steps before you return home:

- ○ Remove your camouflage or disguise (in case there are hunters in the area!).
- ○ Dismantle your trap.
- ○ Take down your tent.
- ○ Pack up your gear and trash.
- ○ Clean up your campsite. Leave the woods exactly as you found them.
- ○ Collect any remaining evidence from the trap now that Bigfoot's gone.

Once you've returned home, record the encounter fully and report it to your Bigfoot club members. You'll also want to share it with the larger Bigfoot community like the Bigfoot Society of America and the Bigfoot Field Researchers Association.

Bigfoot Society of America

This U.S.-based society was established by Morgan Jackson, PhD, and several colleagues. Unlike the invitation-only BFRO, Bigfoot Society of America has membership open to all.

CONCLUSION

You've done it! You caught Bigfoot. You are one of the few, the brave — a true Bigfooter.

Know that there will always be doubters — those who may tease and won't believe you. But don't ever let them stop you from continuing your Bigfoot research! There is still so much to learn and document about these fascinating and elusive creatures — and Bigfoot needs all the supporters it can get! It is our duty to learn as much as we can about this truly endangered species; but also to protect them and their environment.

We must always take care to make sure that these gentle creatures are not exploited and that they are able to continue to live their lives wild and free — just as they always have.

Good luck — and happy Bigfooting!

ANSWERS

PAGES 2-3
1. C, 2. F, 3. B, 4. A, 5. E, 6. D, 7. G

PAGE 4

A. True. Some people believe that *Gigantopithecus* has survived and is known today as Bigfoot.

B. False. After all, they don't bear much physical resemblance, do they?

C. True. Bigfoot and UFOs are often seen at the same time and place. Coincidence?

D. False. That would have to be a very large stuffed animal!

E. True. These early predecessors of modern man did have many Bigfoot-like characteristics: hairy bodies, sloping foreheads, long arms, and large jaws.

F. True. Some people think this. We, of course, know that's not the case.

G. False. Bigfoot has too many unique characteristics to be human. See pages 6–7.

H. True. Unfortunately, people do fear Bigfoot for this reason. See page 14 to find out the truth about Bigfoot's diet.

I. True. This is one of the most prominent theories—that Bigfoot sightings are actually people seeing a bear walking on its hind legs. However, many witnesses insist that what they saw was not a bear!

J. True. Occasionally it happens that someone dresses up as Bigfoot for a prank, but a few people in costume can't explain all the Bigfoot sightings that have occurred across the world for thousands of years!

PAGES 6-7
Head: BF, H; Hair: BF, H; Skin: H, BF; Arms: H, BF; Stomach: BF, H; Legs: H, BF; Feet: BF, H

PAGE 8
Strong   Gentle   Athletic
Bad-smelling   Sensitive   Shy
Curious   Hairy   Good at hiding

PAGE 9

A. False. Bigfoot usually live in small groups with a mother, father, and juvenile.

B. False. Young Bigfoot weigh about 40 pounds when they are born.

C. True. Just like human children, Bigfoot young spend most of their time eating, sleeping, pooping, and crying.

D. False. When a Bigfoot is first born, the mother and baby retreat into a cave for three months.

E. False. Bigfoot babies don't begin to crawl until they're four months old.

F. True. It takes Bigfoot a long time before it learns to walk upright.

G. True. Young Bigfoot are playful and like to test their strength and agility.

PAGES 24-25
1. E, 2. F, 3. A, 4. B, 5. C, 6. D

PAGES 56-57
1. B, 2. C, 3. A

PAGES 26-27

```
O N L M I P E P L E D C C E S X H B W F E Z N K O
E C B O V R F S T W B H W G T Q N F L F E O R R G
M V T I G R Y T E L J F I D S M I L J G E E G F P
D I D M P O O D I R P D G I P M G O V Q D I T L E
U X E L O U E R V S W N G H V S N Y P H H O W L L
N R B Q A G L K E F M N B A F F V L A A E V O V
Y Z T C L A G U C T F R X R R W D I M E E P R L Y
I X B D W H Z R E T S N O M H T R O W E K A D R H
S G B P K P Z Z Y S Y N M N K E D N E P G N A R O
H U I O R G R S O R K G O T D S P D M S U B M J
B C E F H Q F I F E V O M M U B A D U W G I K V S
E M P O J Q N N P M W O J E S S L H N G I H P M
B S U S B S Y C T L Q U K N K Q X I F Y X K O N
S M F A C D S F L R N A V E U E U P O Q T Z B C F
K S W Z D P E W T T E S H N W M A O P Q L C A D P
W H U R R A J B A Q Y L K J K M T D F S E H P B L
V A A Y D Z V I A M Z A V Z E B C R Y C F S R T B
F Q U J F Z N W T C P N R C O V H X C W H R V V A
S C X H S M B N E O G B H Y A S J B U E X V K V
Q S U B A G E T I F Y K O B M S H M I B O C P C F
C V Z N J P T E A T X W M B F P G O Q P L L U A M
R M B N E C A N X D H S M F L F Y A A O T O L I W
H Q V C M R D G G B K L U I Z I Q Y K I D M I H G
R M W U I X X D I A E R Z N S B N Z L N A V P D H
F F A T U V P B Y J B O F S A B P B T S H C K X T
```

PAGE 68

9	8	3	1	7	5	6	4	2
7	2	4	9	3	6	8	1	5
5	6	1	2	4	8	3	9	7
2	1	5	6	9	4	7	8	3
4	3	6	8	1	7	5	2	9
8	7	9	5	2	3	4	6	1
3	5	2	4	6	9	1	7	8
6	9	8	7	5	1	2	3	4
1	4	7	3	8	2	9	5	6

Bibliography & Further Reading

Books:

Burgan, Michael. *The Unexplained: Bigfoot*. Mankato, Minnesota: Capstone Press, 2005.

Cohen, Daniel. *The Encyclopedia of Monsters*. New York: Avon Books, 1991.

Coleman, Loren. *Mysterious America*. Winchester, Massachusetts: Faber & Faber, Inc., 1983.

Floyd, E. Randall. *Great American Mysteries*. Little Rock, Arkansas: House Publishers, 1990.

Gorman, Jacqueline Laks. *Bigfoot*. Milwaukee: Gareth Stevens Publishing, 2002.

Green, John. *Sasquatch: The Apes Among Us*. Seattle: Hancock House Publishers, 1978.

Herbst, Judith. *Monsters*. Minneapolis: Lerner Publications Company, 2005.

Hunter, Don, with René Dahinden. *Sasquatch: The Search for North America's Incredible Creature*. Buffalo, New York: Firefly Books, 1993.

Jackson, Morgan. *So You Want to Catch Bigfoot?* Somerville, Massachusetts: Candlewick Press, 2011.

Meldrum, Jeff. *Sasquatch: Legend Meets Science*. New York: Forge, 2006.

Morgan, Robert W. *Bigfoot Observer's Field Manual*. Enumclaw, Washington: Pine Winds Press, 2008.

Napier, J. *Bigfoot: The Yeti and Sasquatch in Myth and Reality*. New York: E.P. Dutton & Co., 1973.

Woog, Adam. *Mysterious Encounters: Bigfoot*. Farmington Hills, Michigan: Thomson Gale, 2006.

Videos:

Drachkovitch, Rasha, producer. *Ancient Mysteries: Bigfoot* (A&E Network). New York: New Video Group, 1994.

Lee, Julie, and Sheera von Puttkamer, producers. *Sasquatch Odyssey: The Hunt for Bigfoot*. Big Hairy Deal Films, Inc., 1999.

Websites:

Bigfoot Encounters (www.bigfootencounters.com)

Bigfoot Field Researchers Organization (www.bfro.net)

Bigfoot Lives (www.bigfoot-lives.com)

Bigfoot Museum (www.bigfootmuseum.com)

Cryptomundo (www.cryptomundo.com)

The Cryptozoologist (www.lorencoleman.com/cabinet_home.html)

Dean Harrison's Australian Yowie Research (www.yowiehunters.com)

Candlewick Press
99 Dover Street
Somerville, Massachusetts 02144

visit us at www.candlewick.com